Walking through the Jungle

Illustrated by Debbie Harter
Sung by Fred Penner

Barefoot Books
step inside a story

Walking through the jungle,
Walking through the jungle,

Walking through the Jungle

Barefoot Books   Barefoot Books
2067 Massachusetts Ave   29/30 Fitzroy Square
Cambridge, MA 02140   London, W1T 6LQ

First published in Great Britain by Barefoot Books, Ltd

and in the United States of America by Barefoot Books, Inc in 1997

This paperback edition first published in 2011

Graphic design by Tom Grzelinski, Bath, England

Reproduction by B & P International, Hong Kong

Printed in China on 100% acid-free paper by Printplus Ltd

This book was typeset in Architect and One Stroke Script

The illustrations were prepared in paint, pen and ink, and crayon

ISBN 978-1-84686-660-9

British Cataloguing-in-Publication Data:

a catalogue record for this book is available from the British Library

Library of Congress Cataloging-in-Publication Data is available under

LCCN 2004010525

21

Go to *www.barefootbooks.com/junglewalk* to access your
audio singalong and video animation online.

What do you see?
What do you see?

Chasing after me,
Chasing after me.

Floating on the ocean,
Floating on the ocean,

What do you see?
What do you see?

I think I see a whale,

Whoos
Whoos
Whoosh!

Chasing after me,
Chasing after me.

Climbing in the mountains,
Climbing in the mountains,

What do you see?
What do you see?

Chasing after me,
Chasing after me.

Swimming in the river,
Swimming in the river,

What do you see?
What do you see?

Chasing after me,
Chasing after me.

Trekking in the desert,
Trekking in the desert,

What do you see?
What do you see?

Chasing after me,
Chasing after me.

Slipping on the iceberg,
Slipping on the iceberg,

What do you see?
What do you see?

I think I see a polar bear,

Growl!
Growl!
Growl!

Chasing after me,
Chasing after me.

Running home for supper,
Running home for supper,

Where have you been?
Where have you been?

I've been around the world and back,
I've been around the world and back,

And guess what I've seen,
And guess what I've seen.